SESAME STREET

D1543636

Elmo's
Colorful Adventure

Written by Susan Rich Brooke
Illustrated by DiCicco Studios
Original music composed by Paul Heitsch

Read along as Elmo tells you a story. It's all about playing an out-of-this-world game of hide and seek. Elmo loves reading stories with a friend! You will know it's time to turn the page when you hear this sound. . . . Did you hear that? Good! Let's turn the page!

Story Reader

publications international, ltd.

Hi! Welcome to Elmo's World! Elmo's so happy to see you. Oh, and so is Dorothy. Say hello, Dorothy!

Elmo LOVES to draw pictures. He just drew this picture of Baby David. He's Elmo's very favorite doll. Do you have a favorite toy?

Do you want Elmo to tell you more about Baby David? Great! Elmo will go get him.

Hmmm. Elmo's sure Baby David was right here on the table. Baby David?!? Where are you?

Elmo doesn't see Baby David on the table or in the closet or on the floor. Where can he be? Elmo knows! Baby David loves to play games. He must be playing hide and seek!

Hmmm. Maybe Baby David decided not to hide in Elmo's playroom. Maybe he's somewhere else — like deep inside Dorothy's fishbowl! Elmo has always wondered what it's like in there. Do you want to pretend with Elmo and go exploring in Dorothy's fishbowl?

Come on, dive in. The water's fine!

Wow, it's really wet in here! Ooh, and look at all these fish. Dorothy, Elmo had no idea you were so popular!

Elmo sees rocks and coral and plants and an orange drum, but no Baby David. Wait, did Elmo say a DRUM? This looks like the toy drum that Elmo lost last week.

This IS the drum!

So Elmo found something fun, but it isn't Baby David. Elmo doesn't see him anywhere under the water. Elmo wonders — is Baby David ON the water?

Everywhere Elmo looks, he sees blue, like the bright blue sky and the deep blue water. The sky and the water remind Elmo of his favorite crayon. It's called Cookie Monster Blue. Elmo lost it in his backpack.

Wait a minute — isn't that Elmo's blue crayon floating by?

Boy, Elmo thought he would never find his blue crayon! But he still wants to find Baby David.

Elmo has an idea. Maybe Baby David's on a lilypad, just like that little frog. Elmo will hop from lilypad to lilypad to look. Ribbit ribbit. Ribbit ribbit. No Baby David here, or here, or here. Or anywhere! But there IS something over there. Ribbit ribbit.

Hey! It's Elmo's favorite green froggy sunglasses! Elmo thought he lost them!

Elmo found his drum, crayon, and sunglasses in the water. Maybe Elmo will have better luck finding Baby David on land, like here in the place Elmo's imagining now.

Hey, did you know kangaroos hop, just like frogs? Elmo will hippity-hop, too, and look for Baby David. Hippity-hop! Hippity-hop! Hippity-hop!

Elmo sees hills and kangaroos and brown boots, but no Baby David. Hey, wait a minute — what are Elmo's favorite brown boots doing here? He thought he lost them!

Hippity-hop. Hippity-hop. Oh, Elmo's feet are tired from all that hippity-hopping. These boots are really made for flying. Elmo can't find Baby David in the water or on the land, so maybe that means he's up in the sky. Up, up, and away!

Elmo doesn't see Baby David anywhere up here, but look at all the pretty birds. Tweet tweet! Tweet tweet! Elmo sees five birds and one kite. That's the same red kite Elmo lost the other day when he let go of the string!

Birds, a kite — Elmo imagines lots of things flying in the
sky! What do YOU see? Do you see Baby David?

No? Then Elmo will keep looking higher up. He can see lots
of things from way up here, like a black hat in that tree.

Hey, that's Elmo's favorite cowboy hat! He almost didn't
see it, covered with all those butterflies. Elmo's not even going
to think about how it got up HERE!

Hi, butterflies! Can Elmo have his hat back, please? Ah,
thank you!

Elmo's flown so high that he's floating! Can you guess where Elmo is now? That's right, he's in space!

Elmo's looking behind each and every star up here and he still can't find Baby David. But Elmo's found something else — a banana! It's just like the one he left behind in his backpack.

Elmo really wants to find Baby David, but Elmo's happy to find his yummy yellow banana. All this swimming, hopping, flying, and floating has made Elmo hungry.

NOW where is Elmo in space? There are a lot of craters on the ground. Ooh, Elmo knows! He's on the moon! Wow, Elmo can see for miles and miles.

Elmo's pretty sure that Baby David's not up here. Nothing unusual on the moon — except for that white spot over there. It's a baseball! Hey, that's the one Elmo hit out of the ballpark the other day! Zoe said it flew so high it must have landed on the moon. It looks like she was right.

Elmo's back in Elmo's World now. What an adventure! He has been swimming in the water, hopping on the land, flying in the sky, and floating in space. Elmo even walked on the moon! And still Elmo's not found Baby David.

Can you help Elmo, please? Can you think of a place he has not looked, like an iceberg or a deep, dark jungle?

Wait — do you think Elmo should look for Baby David in the TOYBOX?

BABY DAVID! Elmo's so happy he found you! Boy, you missed a really exciting trip in Elmo's imagination. He can't wait to tell you all about it!

Now it's Elmo's turn to hide. Baby David, should we ask our friend to play? Okay! This time, Elmo will hide with Baby David, and YOU—you can find us! Close your eyes and count to ten.

One... two... three...four...five...six...seven...eight...nine...ten!

THE END